HELL

HELL

An Illustrated History of
the Netherworld

R I C H A R D   C R A Z E

CONARI PRESS

Berkeley, CA

Dedicated to

This book is dedicated to Paul Selby, whose devil-
may-care attitude to life has always been such an
inspiration

Copyright © 1996 Conari Press

Text © 1996 Richard Craze
Illustration © 1996 Lorraine Harrison

Originally published by Godsfield Press 1996

DESIGNED AND PRODUCED BY
THE BRIDGEWATER BOOK COMPANY LTD
Picture research by Venessa Fletcher

The author and publishers are grateful to the following for the use of illustrations:
Bridgeman Art Library, e.t.archive, Giraudon/Bridgeman, Images Colour Library,
Tate Gallery, London.

For information, contact:
Conari Press,
2550 Ninth St., Suite 101,
Berkeley, CA 94710

Printed and bound in Singapore by Tien Wah Press

Conari Press books are distributed by Publishers Group West.

Library of Congress Cataloging-in-Publication Data

Craze, Richard, 1950–
          Hell: an illustrated history of the netherworld/by Richard
Craze.
          p.   cm.
Includes bibliographical references and Index.
ISBN 1-57324-059-1
1. Hell—Cooperative studies.   2. Hell—Humor.   I. Title
BL545.C73 1996
291.2'3—dc20 96-5974
CIP

CONTENTS

INTRODUCTION

*V*IRTUALLY EVERY CULTURE has evolved a mythology to explain what happens to the human soul after death, as well as a mythology to explain in some way natural phenomena such as storms and floods – powerful gods of chaos. Mythology is just another word for religion, usually applied to ancient religions, although it could also apply to more modern ones. Different cultures have developed different ideas of hell for various reasons, including: to explain what happens after death; to motivate people to lead a good life for spiritual ends; to control people politically by frightening them with a threat of damnation or torture; or to incorporate a sense of justice. A culture's view of hell may be one of these or a combination of several.

EVERY COMPASSION, EVERY GRACE, EVERY SPARING, EVERY LAST TRACE OF CONSIDERATION FOR THE INCREDULOUS, IMPLORING OBJECTION "THAT YOU VERILY CANNOT DO SO UNTO A SOUL": IT IS DONE, IT HAPPENS, AND INDEED WITHOUT BEING CALLED TO ANY RECKONING IN WORDS; IN SOUNDLESS CELLAR, FAR DOWN BENEATH GOD'S HEARING, AND HAPPENS TO ALL ETERNITY.

Thomas Mann
Dr. Faustus

Primitive cultures evolve creation myths to explain how the world and people came into being, and they usually also have local deities whom they worship for protection, placation, and to ensure a good supply of food. Early people lived as hunter-gatherers and, as such, were far more prey to the laws of chance than the farming people who succeeded them. Hunting is a risky business – fail to find enough game and the whole tribe suffers. Local deities would usually be visually represented as the animals that the tribe were hunting – often depicted as

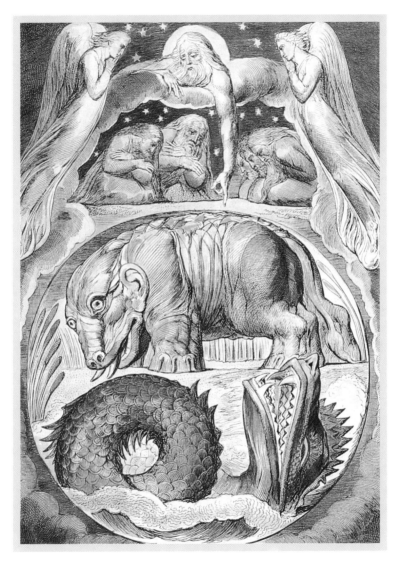

BEHEMOTH AND LEVIATHAN
William Blake 1757–1827

horned – as a form of sympathetic or animal magic. These horned gods played no part in the afterlife but were there merely to provide a source of predictable food.

Some of the earliest examples of these horned gods are to be found in the cave paintings of Trois-Frères in southern France. They were painted by Paleolithic (early Stone Age) people during the Pleistocene period. They depict a magician-priest with a bison's head, cloven hooves, and an upright man's body. They are dancing and playing bowed musical instruments.

Around 5,000 years before the birth of Christ, hunting gave way to farming and agricultural civilizations were born – mainly in Mesopotamia. A completely different type of mythology was now called for – one that relied less on chance and more on order and planning. A whole new pantheon of gods was born – gods to whom the people could appeal for regular and bountiful harvests. These new gods related more closely to the life-giving sun and were more intimately connected to the afterlife – the whole mythology of death and rebirth makes more sense to farmers, who rely heavily on the seasons, than to hunters, who can follow the wild herds.

Once a new hierarchy of brighter, more ordered gods had been established there remained the problem of what to do with the old gods. They could not be killed off in case they contained a residue of power, so they had to be demoted – relegated to being custodians of some dark netherworld. In the new order, heaven was the life-giving sky, so it made sense that its opposite must lie below – in the ground. And so the old horned gods of the Stone Age people became the new rulers of hell.

There was a sort of logic in locating the place of the dead below ground – the underworld – because that was exactly where the dead were buried. And if the soul was immortal, it made sense to believe that it rose upward – to the sky and the sun.

It seems that the more "civilized" a culture is, the more its concept of hell reflects that culture. For example, the Native American peoples only have a concept of heaven – the Happy Hunting Grounds. When someone dies they go to a better place, where there is always plentiful food and comfortable living. The Chinese, on the other hand, have at least eighteen complex levels of hell, reflecting the hierarchical class system of China itself. The Aboriginal peoples of Australia have only the Dreamtime, a form of heaven, and no concept of hell, whereas Christians have evolved complex systems of hell, heaven, purgatory, and even limbo. Most African tribes have no concept of hell. The Buddha declared that there was no such thing as hell, but Buddhists themselves believe that there are many different hells, each with its own punishments and tortures.

Perhaps primitive people did not need a concept of hell because they had little in the way of sin. The more complex a culture becomes, the more openings there are for sin and immorality.

In this book we explore some of these concepts of hell and look at some of its rulers – the horned gods of the Stone Age. We may not need to believe in hell any more, but it can still be a positive and motivating concept to remind us that we are spiritual beings who need to rise ever upward toward the heavens.

THE GEOGRAPHY OF HELL

WHERE IS HELL?

$\mathcal{E}$very culture that has a concept of hell locates it in a different place, although most agree that hell lies somewhere underground, beneath or in the earth. Some beliefs actually extend the location to the whole of the earth itself. The Gnostic Cathars, for instance, believed that God lived a long way away and that this earth was actually created by the Devil. They believed that everything here is corrupted by evil and that we are already living through hell. Even simple pleasures are the Devil's work and are not to be enjoyed. For this heresy they were not very popular with the Church and were burnt. There are still a great many people who believe that this life is hell – we are already in it – and that heaven will be the afterlife. Buddhists mainly believe in reincarnation – there is no heaven or hell, only a perpetual cycle of birth and rebirth – yet some Buddhists have their own idea of hell, that has so many tortures that, it is said, it would take 100,000 years merely to describe them all.

The Mayans of South America, on the other hand, did not believe in hell at all as a place; for them it was certain periods of time. They believed that there were nine hells, each lasting fifty-two years, and that hell only began in 1519, coinciding with the arrival of the white man. Their hell was an absence of Mayans and should have finished in 1987, when they predicted that a new Mayan age would begin.

The Swahili hell is a vast seven-floored building that exists under the earth, and the Native Americans' concept of hell was an underworld of shadowy ghosts and shades – they went there if (like the Vikings) they did not die in glorious battle.

Emanuel Swedenborg of Stockholm was an inventor and scientist in the eighteenth century who claimed he had visited hell. He said he went down in a brass elevator and found two levels of hell. The first was dark and filled with the spirits of evil, and the second was bright with hell-fire and the souls of the tormented. He describes the first as if it were an inner city with lanes and streets: "and within these hovels infernal spirits engage in continuous altercations, displays of enmity, beatings, and tear one another to pieces. There are brothels disgusting to behold, being full of all sorts of filth and excrement."

Swedenborg described his experiences in his book *Heaven and Hell,* which most people took quite literally.

WHAT IN THE MIDST LAY
BUT THE TOWER ITSELF?
THE ROUND SQUAT
TURRET, BLIND AS THE
FOOL'S HEART,
BUILT OF BROWN STONE,
WITHOUT A
COUNTERPART
IN THE WHOLE WORLD.

Robert Browning
Childe Roland to the
Dark Tower Came

WHAT IS HELL?

*H*ELL IS INVARIABLY a place of punishment and torture. Each culture has a set of laws or rules for people to live by. Breaking these rules, or failing to live up to a certain standard of morality, would be sufficient to cause someone to be sent to hell, and their punishment there would be allocated according to the severity of their sins.

Medieval Christians were very concerned with the Seven Deadly Sins, and sinners of each of these sins were to suffer a particular punishment in hell.

The prideful were to be broken on the wheel – they were tied on vast wheels, which were turned over hell-fires while demons tormented them. The envious were immersed in freezing water. The gluttonous were force-fed by demons on toads, snakes, and rats. The ambitious were boiled in vast vats of boiling oil, while demons forced their heads below the surface. The slothful were thrown into snake-pits and were pushed down into them every time they tried to escape. The angry were dismembered alive, while the traditional hell-fire and brimstone were reserved for the lustful.

> NO, NO, NO, MY CHILD: DO NOT PRAY. IF YOU DO, YOU WILL THROW AWAY THE MAIN ADVANTAGE OF THIS PLACE. WRITTEN OVER THE GATE HERE ARE THE WORDS "LEAVE EVERY HOPE BEHIND, YE WHO ENTER." ONLY THINK WHAT A RELIEF THAT IS! FOR WHAT IS HOPE? A FORM OF MORAL RESPONSIBILITY. HERE THERE IS NO HOPE, AND CONSEQUENTLY NO DUTY, NO WORK, NOTHING TO BE GAINED BY PRAYING, NOTHING TO BE LOST BY DOING WHAT YOU LIKE. HELL, IN SHORT, IS A PLACE WHERE YOU HAVE NOTHING TO DO BUT AMUSE YOURSELF.
>
> *George Bernard Shaw*
> Man and Superman

DETAIL OF HELL FROM THE LAST JUDGEMENT
Fra Angelico c.1387–1455

DANTE'S INFERNO

*D*ANTE WAS BORN in Florence in 1265 and his real name was Durante Alighieri. He was the son of a notary and had a good education, learning classical Greek and Latin. As a young man he wrote poetry, mainly about love, and became a pharmacist, a magistrate, and an elected town official. These were the days of intrigue and rivalry and while Dante was in Rome on official business his political enemies rose up and took control of the city. Dante was banished and warned never to return to Florence. He became an exile, although his wife and children were allowed to stay there, and he wandered throughout Europe, where he began work on the three books of his *Divine Comedy*. The word "comedy" in the title did not imply humor in those days; merely that the story would end happily. The three books were about an imaginary journey through hell, purgatory, and heaven and were published after his death in 1321. Did Dante actually visit these places, as many people thought? Were they visions or dreams? Moral epics? Dante himself said that they came to him in a vision, but that was what a lot of writers said about their work then — it gave it an air of authority. The three books of *The Divine Comedy* can be read on many different levels. They do have a vision-like quality about them; they are also great poetic works, and wickedly biting satires.

Dante describes hell as a deep funnel-shaped cavity with round circular sides, on which are built great terraces with steep drops down to the next. Down these sheer cliff faces flow four rivers, towards the very center of hell, where there is the bottomless burning lake of the Evil One. These rivers are the Styx, the river of hate; Acheron, the river of sorrow; Phlegethon, the river of fire; and Lethe, the river of forgetfulness. These are the same rivers that are mentioned in classic Greek and Romans myths (see pages 52–55 and 58–59).

THE INSCRIPTION OVER THE GATE
William Blake 1757–1827

The story starts with Dante lost in a dark wood. The Roman poet Virgil rescues him and they approach the huge gates that mark the entrance to hell, whose inscription reads:

> *Through me you pass into the city of woe: Through me you pass into eternal pain: Through me among the people lost for aye... All hope abandon, ye who enter here.*

When Dante and Virgil first enter they find a great multitude of people milling about. These, Virgil explains, are the ones who in life could never make decisions – they are not wicked enough for hell and they never did anything worthy enough for heaven, so they are doomed forever to mill about in a sort of limbo for waverers.

As Dante wanders through hell who should he see there being tortured and punished but his old enemies from Florence, as well as the souls of those who on earth chose to live evil lives of pleasure.

The two go down through the nine levels of hell and see the various tortures, which include: rushing gales of wind blowing in all directions; a continual storm of rain, hail, and snow from which shelter is denied; rolling heavy weights about (which Dante presumably borrowed from the Greek myth of Sisyphus, see page 52); living in marshes and bogs; rending and tearing other spirits in mud; suicides being imprisoned in shrubs and bushes; people living on a plain of burning sand in a perpetual sand storm; having heavy weights tied around their necks; and being bespattered with mire and having to live in a lair. The whole place is dark and brutish, and filled with the screams and anguish of the condemned, and Dante and Virgil finally escape with only the merest glimpse of Satan himself – just enough to see that he is still clutching the tormented body of Judas.

Dante next visits purgatory and heaven. In purgatory he is again guided by Virgil, but his visit to heaven is supervised by Beatrice, his childhood sweetheart.

THE HELL OF REINCARNATION

*T*HE HINDUS OF INDIA believe in a very different hell from that of other cultures such as Christianity – theirs is a hell of the here and now rather than some other place of punishment and torture

The Indian *Bhagavad Gita* ("The Song of the Lord"), a holy book like the Bible, is a description of the teachings of Lord Krishna to the warrior prince Arjuna, his disciple. Krishna says that hell has three gateways – lust, greed, and anger. If people fall into the trap of these three destructive evils they are condemned to the hell of this life on earth. However, if they practise what is good for them they will be liberated from these three gates to darkness and will go to the Supreme Good. But the Hindu heaven is not a permanent state – people only stay there for as long as their merits last. Merits are built up during life for all the good deeds they do. Once their merits run out, they have to come back and be reborn into another life here – reincarnation.

Krishna, who is the eighth "avatar," or representation of the God Vishnu on earth, says that by practising yoga one can be freed from the hell of this life, because it purifies the self. One should also be friendly and compassionate, balanced in pleasure and pain, and patient.

Anyone not adhering to this lifestyle will be given over to egotism, power, insolence, lust, and wrath. Krishna went on to say:

...these malicious people hate Me in their own bodies and those of others. These worst among men, evil doers in the world, I hurl forever into the wombs of the demons [the asurisu]. Entering into demonic wombs the deluded ones, in birth after birth without ever reaching Me, will fall into a condition still lower [Narake — hell]... ignorance is the instigator inducing man to indulge in all three of the triple gates to hell — lust, greed, and anger. When these three evils are eliminated the path of enlightenment opens and the darkness of ignorance vanishes of its own accord. When the demonical man takes to the divine way his progress is very rapid. A zealous convert that he is, he hastens quickly Godward.

NOW AND AGAIN THE DULL, THE GENTLE DAMNED
    STIR, AND SOME SALVAGED LUCIFER WILL TRY
TO ORGANIZE REVOLT. WHICH HEAVEN DOES NOT MIND.
    WHAT DOES IT MEAN? A FEW LOST SPIRITS CLUTCHING
CHARRED BANNERS WITH THE MOTTO "WE WANT WINGS,"
    OR "HARPS FOR HELL," OR "GOLDEN CROWNS FOR ALL."
THE UNPRESENTABLE, SCRAP-HEAP LUCIFER FLINGS
    A WRITTEN PROTEST OVER HEAVEN'S WALL.
"THEY'RE BOUND TO ANSWER," "THIS TIME THEY MUST DO SOMETHING" —
    THE MEEK SPIRITS WHISPER, WAITING OUTSIDE. HOURS GO BY.
SUDDENLY A TERRIBLE LIGHT
FLASHES OVER THEM. IS IT SOME NEW DEVICE
FOR BLISTERING HELL — FOR CUTTING OFF THEIR RETREAT?
    NO! THAT TRANSCENDENT WHITENESS IS THE ANGEL OF THE DAY
TELLING THEM QUIETLY BUT FIRMLY TO GO AWAY.

Arthur Waley No Discharge

To Hindus, being trapped forever in the cycle of rebirth is their idea of hell; to be outside the love of Vishnu in any of His forms is a living hell from which one must strive to escape. By devotion to God, practising yoga, and reading the holy scriptures we can again find our rightful place at the Lord's side, and be freed from this life.

Why do the Hindus see this life as a living hell? Well, to them this world is one of suffering and pain, and any sense they may have of enjoyment or pleasure is only temporary. They describe this life as bewildered by many a fancy, enmeshed in the snare of delusion, and by living, people are addicted to the gratification of lust. Hindus believe that people are not really happy at all – they only think they are happy because they have not been able to see through the illusion of this life. People think that the pain, disappointments, and failures of this life are just misfortunes, when they should recognize that they are actually lessons sent to turn them from the path of delusion and back to the love of God – they are the punishments of hell, already present before death.

To Hindus there is no judgement in any of this. Anyone can instantly become saved merely by following the rules laid down by Krishna. They can begin at any time of their lives – although if they leave it too late, they will be unable to build up much in the way of merits. In order to amass an inexhaustible supply of merits, all they need do is live a life in which they have not made a single mistake.

WAR, OR THE RIDE TO DISCORD *Henri Rousseau* 1844–1910

THE CHARACTERS OF HELL

THE GODDESS HEL

*T*HE VIKINGS were Scandinavians who set out across the North Sea to pillage and plunder around 900 A.D. They were a warrior race with a complex pantheon of gods and goddesses.

THERE ARE TWO EQUAL AND OPPOSITE ERRORS INTO WHICH OUR RACE CAN FALL ABOUT THE DEVILS. ONE IS TO DISBELIEVE IN THEIR EXISTENCE. THE OTHER IS TO BELIEVE, AND TO FEEL AN EXCESSIVE AND UNHEALTHY INTEREST IN THEM. THEY THEMSELVES ARE EQUALLY PLEASED BY BOTH ERRORS AND HAIL A MATERIALIST OR A MAGICIAN WITH THE SAME DELIGHT.

C.S. Lewis
The Screwtape Letters

In Viking mythology, hell is ruled over by the goddess Hel and her kingdom is Niflheim (icy world of the dead). Hel is an unpleasant character, in common with the rest of her family. Her father was Loki, the Viking god of wickedness; her mother was the giantess Angrboda; her eldest brother was the wolf Fenrir, who was later to swallow the whole earth and bring the world to an end at Ragnarok – "his slavering mouth will gape wide open, so wide his jaws will scrape the

earth and sky, flames will dance in his eyes and leap from his nostrils." And Hel's younger brother was Jormungand, greatest of all the serpents, who would help Fenrir at Ragnarok by spewing forth venom; "all the earth will be splashed and stained with his poison."

The other gods of Viking mythology disliked Hel from the start and asked the Norns, the three wise crones of Fate, Being, and Necessity, what could be done about her. The Norns said that since her father was Loki, the Father of Lies, there was not much that could be done. They suggested that she never be

IN THE REALM OF HEL
19th-century book illustration

given a chance and that all three children be captured. Fenrir was bound in an unbreakable chain made from a woman's beard, the sound a cat makes when it walks, the sinews of a bear, a fish's breath, a bird's spit, and the roots of a mountain. Jormungand was thrown into the ocean, where he grew so big that he encircled the entire world with his tail in his mouth.

But what could be done about Hel? Odin, chief god of the Vikings, threw her out of Asgard, the Viking heaven, and banished her to the darkness and mist of the ice world, Niflheim, the world below worlds.

Odin told her that she could look after the dead – not the warriors, she did not get those, but only those who had died of illness, old age, or had been criminals. And she had to share any food she managed to get with them. She was not too pleased and resolved to join her two brothers at Ragnarok at the end of time. In the meantime she was obliged to wait in Niflheim, which she turned into a foul fortress. Once dead and handed over to her, a soul had no chance of escape and was condemned to wait in the icy darkness with her. There was not much to eat – in fact she called her plate "Hunger" and her knife "Famine" – and there was not much to do. In fact, time went so slowly

THOR BATTLING WITH JORMUNGAND
19th-century book illustration

that no one could tell if anyone else was actually moving.

From the waist up Hel looked normal – but from the waist down she was all rotting and decayed flesh, greenish-black. Her face was grim as well – she was never once known to smile, and just one look from her was enough to cause continual vomiting.

I AM THY FATHER'S SPIRIT,
  DOOMED FOR A CERTAIN TERM TO WALK THE NIGHT,
    AND FOR THE DAY CONFINED TO FAST IN FIRES,
TILL THE FOUL CRIMES DONE IN MY DAYS OF NATURE
  ARE BURNT AND PURGED AWAY. BUT THAT I AM FORBID
    TO TELL THE SECRETS OF MY PRISON HOUSE,
I COULD A TALE UNFOLD WHOSE LIGHTEST WORD
  WOULD HARROW UP THY SOUL, FREEZE THY YOUNG BLOOD,
    MAKE THY TWO EYES LIKE STARS START FROM THEIR SPHERES.

William Shakespeare Hamlet

All in all, Niflheim was not a very pleasant experience. The only people who avoided going there were warriors who died in battle or women who went to the goddess of love and fertility at Freyja's Fortress. Everyone else went to Hel — forever. At least until Ragnarok. And when that time came they were destined only to be used as ballast in a vast ship that Hel would have built.

In Niflheim there was no chance of redemption or escape. There was nothing anyone could do to atone for the sin of dying of old age or disease. And there was no way of physically escaping, for Hel guarded Niflheim with a giant hound, the monstrous Garm, who patrolled ceaselessly, his mouth and throat caked with the dried blood of those who tried to flee. So the early Christians borrowed Hel's name for their own place of punishment.

THE DEVIL

*A*S EACH HELL reflects the belief system of a culture, so too does the portrayal of the ruler of hell – whom we will call the Devil. In mythology the Devil is invariably a representation of the earlier god or gods of a culture – those who cannot be disposed of entirely, merely demoted and sent to the underworld themselves.

BY THY COLD BREAST AND SERPENT SMILE,
BY THY UNFATHOM'D GULFS OF GUILE,
BY THAT MOST SEEMING VIRTUOUS EYE,
BY THY SHUT SOUL'S HYPOCRISY;
BY THE PERFECTION OF THINE ART
WHICH PASS'D FOR HUMAN THINE OWN
HEART;
BY THY DELIGHT IN OTHERS' PAIN,
AND BY THY BROTHERHOOD OF CAIN,
I CALL UPON THEE! AND COMPEL
THYSELF TO BE THY PROPER HELL!

Lord Byron
Manfred

The Satan portrayed in Milton's *Paradise Lost* was the arch-rebel, the individualist, capable both of reasoning and emotion. He initially regrets his actions, that have led him, and his fallen angels, to be thrown out of heaven – he feels he cannot let them down. So he is obliged to take up his role as tempter and tormentor, but he does it laconically and with great sophistication.

So who is the real Satan? In the Bible, the word "Satan" means adversary, and that was how he was known for the first 300 years of Christianity. It was not until around 590 A.D. (the time of Pope Gregory the Great) that his name was even finally settled. Until then he had been called Satanel, Lucifer (Lord of Light), Belial (The Worthless), Mastema (The Great Enemy), Beelzeboul (Lord of Excrement), Beelzebub (Lord of Flies), and

Azazel (Lord of the Wasteland). These were older gods from cultures with which the early Christians came into contact, or they were Hebrew deities.

To give Satan a visual representation, the early Christians borrowed heavily from earlier mythologies, and the generally accepted appearance of Satan is an amalgamation of such things as the horns and shaggy hindquarters of the Greek god Pan, the wings of the Mesopotamian devil Pazuzu, and the scales and dragon skin of the Persian Azhidaahaka.

Once given an identity, Satan's power surged until his heyday in the Middle Ages, when death parades and mystery plays were very popular. They took the same theme over and over again – the temptation of Man and his descent into hell. With the plague and other catastrophes, people began to worry more about dying than about what happened to them afterwards, and the Devil's power began to

> HOW YOU HAVE FALLEN FROM HEAVEN, BRIGHT MORNING STAR, FELLED TO THE EARTH, SPRAWLING HELPLESS ACROSS THE NATIONS! YOU THOUGHT IN YOUR OWN MIND, I WILL SCALE THE HEAVENS...YET SHALL YOU BE BROUGHT DOWN TO SHEOL, TO THE DEPTHS OF THE ABYSS.
>
> Isaiah 14:12

flicker and wane. By the 1600s the most popular image was the skeleton, rather than the horned demon of the medieval period. The Devil had become a mere shadow of his former self. During the 1700s, the Age of Reason, most people believed that the sun was the most likely setting for hell, and the power of the Devil was reduced to the sardonic grin of the skull.

It can be revealing to look at other hellish characters to see what similarities they have and how they are invariably earlier gods who have been demoted.

HELLISH CHARACTERS

*B*EELZEBUB was originally the god of the Philistines. Jehovah, god of the Israelites, told his people to stop the Philistines worshipping Beelzebub. The Philistines wanted to know why. The Israelites said that it was because he was not important enough – he was only a god of little things, like flies and other bugs. Thus he became Beelzebub, Lord of Flies. His name is often used as another name for Satan although Milton, in his *Paradise Lost*, makes him Satan's assistant.

WHY THIS IS HELL,
NOR AM I OUT OF IT:
THINKST THOU THAT I WHO
SAW THE FACE OF GOD
AND TASTED THE ETERNAL
JOYS OF HEAVEN,
AM NOT TORMENTED WITH
TEN THOUSAND HELLS
IN BEING DEPRIVED OF
EVERLASTING BLISS!

Christopher Marlowe
Dr. Faustus

Xipetotec was the Aztec god of pain, which he liked so much that he even flayed himself alive – hence his name, which means "flayed Lord." He is Mictlantecuhtli's main helper when it comes to torturing souls and is also responsible for inflicting disease, plague, and madness on the living. Most of the human sacrifices were made to him to appease his need to inflict pain. Slaves would have been flayed and the Aztec priests would have worn their skins in imitation of Xipetotec. His followers also attempted to flay their own skin using thorns from cactus plants.

MICTLANTECUHTLI, AZTEC GOD OF HELL AND DEATH

Kali is the wicked side of the Hindu goddess Devi. She was sent to earth to battle with a plague of demons. However, she was overcome with blood-lust and slew everyone around her – including her consort Shiva. Her name means the "black destroyer" and she is usually depicted as having four arms and holding a severed head, a sword, a holy book, and a rosary. She wears a necklace of human skulls and a belt of severed arms.

Moloch was the god of the Canaanites. He is usually portrayed as an old man with horns, who has children sacrificed to him, whom he then burns. In Carthage he was worshipped as Baal-Hammon, and the Hebrews took him over to become their Satan.

Pan was the Greek god of nature. He was not originally a devil but has increasingly been seen as one. We get the word "panic" from the reaction of meeting him face to face. He was more licentious than wicked, although he could be bad-tempered and irritable.

Rashnu was the Persian god of the dead. The soul had to wait for three days and nights while Rashnu weighed up its life. If he considered it worthy, it could cross over the narrow bridge to heaven – assisted by a nubile young maiden. But if it had led a life of debauchery and wickedness, then it was consigned to hell – across the same narrow bridge, although it became so narrow that it was sharper than a razor blade. The wicked always fell off the bridge into the yawning pits of the abyss below, where frightful demons were waiting to devour them. Rashnu had a reputation for being scrupulously fair – he could not be bribed, tricked, or argued with.

Mara was originally a devil of the Hindus, who was known as "the

MARA, THE TEMPTER AND ARCH-FIEND

destroyer." He was the ruler of the underworld and was the devil who tempted the Buddha as he sat reaching enlightenment. Mara sent his three daughters to dance before the Buddha and seduce him. When this did not work, he sent a party of demons to frighten him. This did not work either, so Mara threw bolts of fire at the Buddha's head. The Buddha ignored these as well and Mara was defeated. He is now regarded as the one who tempts Buddhists away from asceticism.

Shiva is husband to Kali. He is just as terrible, although quite handsome, despite having four arms and four faces, with three eyes in each. He wears snakes round his head, skulls round his neck, and frequents graveyards, keeping company with a pack of bloodthirsty demons.

Ahriman was the Persian god of chaos. He was seen as not so much leading the good astray as encouraging fools. The god of light and goodness, Ahura Mazda, was his brother, and the two have competed for souls since the dawn of time. Ahriman won the souls of liars, cheats, and fools, whom he then tormented by ridiculing. He was also credited with creating the three-headed dragon, Azhidaahaka, who let loose pain, misery, and death.

The Antichrist is the supposed son of Satan, who will be born just before the Last Judgement. He is seen as the antithesis of Jesus – come to lead us all into trouble. Just about every tyrant during the last two thousand years, including Napoleon, has been suspected of being the Antichrist, but it is likely that he has not yet arrived.

Mot was the Lord of Death of the Canaanites. He was responsible for the death, every autumn, of Baal, the good god, by making him eat poisoned mud. In the spring Baal killed Mot and returned above ground. Because Baal had to spend the winter in the underworld he became confused with Mot and is now seen as an early form of Beelzebub.

Erlik was the Siberian ruler of the underworld. Legend has it that he was actually the first man to be created (his name means "father") and while the other people were being created (but before they had souls) Erlik spat on them out of jealousy and spite. Ulgan, the god of creation, was not too pleased. Apparently he had to turn us inside-out, which is why we look so ugly to this day. As a punishment, Erlik was given the underworld to rule, which delighted him as it contains more dead souls than living ones.

APOCALYPSE
Albrecht Dürer 1471–1528

Ghede – more popularly known as Baron Samedi – is the Voodoo god of death. He wears a black top hat and tail-coat, and half his face is frequently white. Nowadays he is usually portrayed wearing dark glasses as well. As god of death, his job is protecting the dead from grave-robbers,

E SPIRIT
EVIL AND
LL

although he has often been known to turn the dead into zombies. Ghede is benevolent unless he is given access to rum, of which the merest taste makes him unpredictable and dangerous.

Ictinike was the trickster devil of the Sioux of North America. He was not so much a ruler of hell as a tormentor of the living. His principal trick was to persuade the first people to let him wear their fur skins for a while (people were originally a kind of giant rabbit) and he would then not give the fur back. Consequently we are still naked to this day.

Tiamat was the Babylonian female dragon devil. She was created before time began and ruled the universe. To begin with she was good, but the other gods angered her and she became monstrous. She was challenged to battle by Marduk, bull of the Sun. He defeated her by hurling a storm into her mouth and a lance into her belly. After she died he cut up her body and made the earth and heavens from it. According to Babylonian myth, people are basically wicked because they were created from Tiamat.

In Greek mythology Kronos was the youngest son of the Titan giants. He was warned that one of his children might depose him, so he ate them at birth. Zeus, his youngest child, escaped and hurled Kronos into the pit, Tartarus, where he became ruler of hell.

Mephistopheles was invented in medieval times as a sophisticated version of Satan. He is the wily tempter who persuades Faustus to sell his soul.

DEMONS ARMED WITH STICKS
Mathias Grünewald 1455–1528

ℋOW TO GET INTO (AND OUT OF) HELL

$\mathcal{T}$HE CULTURES that have a concept of hell usually have a complex and ritualistic set of procedures for getting out of hell. The Chinese believe that if someone ends up in hell, then only by their descendants burning money can they be bribed out – or if someone has died an unnatural death, they can trick someone else into taking their place. Christians believe that once someone is confined to hell there is no escape or redemption, whereas Buddhists believe that even if someone does end up in hell there is always a chance of redemption if the unfortunate sinner calls upon the Buddha himself to save him. The truly repentant will be liberated.

Getting into hell is usually fairly easy. Each culture has its own moral code and, by failing to live up to it, sinners sentence themselves to eternal hell.

> IT DOES NOT MATTER HOW SMALL THE SINS ARE PROVIDED THAT THEIR CUMULATIVE EFFECT IS TO EDGE THE MAN AWAY FROM THE LIGHT AND OUT INTO THE NOTHING. MURDER IS NO BETTER THAN CARDS IF CARDS CAN DO THE TRICK. INDEED THE SAFEST ROAD TO HELL IS THE GRADUAL ONE – THE GENTLE SLOPE, SOFT UNDERFOOT, WITHOUT SUDDEN TURNINGS, WITHOUT MILESTONES, WITHOUT SIGNPOSTS.
>
> *C.S. Lewis*
> The Screwtape Letters

THE DAMNED IN HELL
Master of Palantes Altar late 15th century

THE HARROWING OF HELL

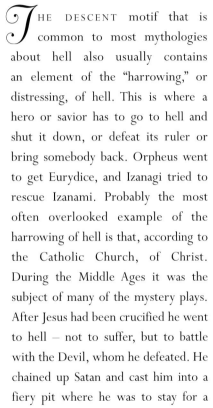

THE DESCENT motif that is common to most mythologies about hell also usually contains an element of the "harrowing," or distressing, of hell. This is where a hero or savior has to go to hell and shut it down, or defeat its ruler or bring somebody back. Orpheus went to get Eurydice, and Izanagi tried to rescue Izanami. Probably the most often overlooked example of the harrowing of hell is that, according to the Catholic Church, of Christ. During the Middle Ages it was the subject of many of the mystery plays. After Jesus had been crucified he went to hell — not to suffer, but to battle with the Devil, whom he defeated. He chained up Satan and cast him into a fiery pit where he was to stay for a thousand years. As well as closing down hell, Jesus rescued Adam and other ancient souls, who were redeemed. Ignoring the pleas of the truly wicked,

THE DESCENT
INTO ANNWN

he set the sign of the cross in the middle of hell and came back to be resurrected. He therefore both symbolically defeated death and literally defeated evil. This is what the line in the Apostle's Creed in the Prayer Book of 1662 is about – "He descended into Hell, the third day he arose again from the dead."

According to tradition, Jesus is supposed to have closed hell completely and it is to stay that way for a thousand years. Jesus comes back with the keys of hell and it is locked up for good. However, this caused problems both for theologians and for believers. If hell is closed, what happens to the souls of the wicked? The early Christians were now obliged to introduce the concept of a sort of waiting-room, where souls would stay for the thousand years until hell was open again. They found a ready-made idea – limbo – that they freely borrowed from the Romans, who had borrowed it from the Greeks. Limbo became a place where anyone who did not quite fit could be put. All the characters of the Old Testament could be interred here – they could not go to heaven because they were Jewish, but they had not necessarily done anything wrong (besides which, hell was closed anyway). The souls of unbaptized children could also go there – and respected figures from ancient history, like Plato.

I BELIEVE IN GOD THE FATHER ALMIGHTY, MAKER OF HEAVEN AND EARTH: AND IN JESUS CHRIST HIS ONLY SON OUR LORD, WHO WAS CONCEIVED BY THE HOLY GHOST, BORN OF THE VIRGIN MARY, SUFFERED UNDER PONTIUS PILATE, WAS CRUCIFIED, DEAD AND BURIED, HE DESCENDED INTO HELL; THE THIRD DAY HE AROSE FROM THE DEAD, HE ASCENDED INTO HEAVEN, AND SITTETH ON THE RIGHT HAND OF GOD THE FATHER ALMIGHTY; FROM THENCE HE SHALL COME TO JUDGE THE QUICK AND THE DEAD.

Prayer Book 1662

This was all fine until around the year 1000 A.D., when Satan's banishment was supposed to end. Obviously something went wrong, because Satan was expected to reappear with his son, the Antichrist, and the end of the world would take place. But nothing happened. The theologians set to work and said that Satan was now out and about in the world – tempting and tormenting – and that hell was still closed but that there was another place where sinners would be punished. This was purgatory. It was a cross between limbo and hell. But if Satan was absent, who was to run it? Jesus' mother, the Virgin Mary, was called back from heaven, where she had been asleep (the Dormition). She was given the keys of hell to look after, and the running of purgatory. She does not administer any punishments – in fact, her main job seems to be protecting the souls of the sinners from the wrath of her son. Purgatory became a sort of temporary hell – but one from which sinners could be rescued. Indeed, they could take action to prevent themselves being assigned there in the first place by buying an "indulgence." These were sold by the Church and saved sinners from the results of their sins, guaranteeing that they went to heaven when they died. Until Christ himself went to heaven, there was no one there (according to Christian theology) except God and the angels – everyone else who had died previously having gone to hell. Christ's harrowing of hell was probably essential, both to close it down and to free some space for future souls.

DANTE AND VIRGIL APPROACHING THE ANGEL
WHO GUARDS THE GATE OF PURGATORY
William Blake 1757–1827

THE TRIUMPH
OF
DEATH
*Pieter Brueghel
the Elder*
1525–69

THE DESCENT MOTIF

*O*NE OF THE most common aspects of the mythology of hell is that it is a place where nature goes in the winter. Nature is usually represented as a god or goddess. Come the winter, with its cold and hardships, it is easy to believe that hell has somehow taken over. What is invariably needed is someone to go down to the underworld and rescue nature, so that spring can return to the land. This is known as "the descent motif" and it crops up in many mythologies about hell. Some of these descent motifs are explored in the section on the Ancient Visions of Hell (pages 50–65).

> HELL HATH NO LIMITS NOR IS CIRCUMSCRIB'D
> IN ONE SELF PLACE, WHERE WE ARE IS HELL,
> AND WHERE HELL IS, THERE WE MUST EVER BE.
> AND TO BE SHORT, WHEN ALL THE WORLD DISSOLVES,
> AND EVERY CREATURE SHALL BE PURIFIED,
> ALL PLACES SHALL BE HELL THAT ARE NOT HEAVEN.
>
> *Christopher Marlowe* Dr. Faustus

ARTHUR IN THE GRUESOME GLEN
Henry Clarence Whaite 1828–1912

ANCIENT VISIONS OF HELL

THE BABYLONIAN HELL

MOST HISTORIANS agree that the birth of true civilization occurred in the fertile valley that is found between the rivers of the Tigris and the Euphrates – the area known as Mesopotamia – around 4000 B.C. This is also where the Garden of Eden is said to have been located.

The Mesopotamian civilizations began with the Sumerians, followed by the Phoenicians, the Carthaginians, and the Babylonians. Each borrowed heavily from each other mythologically, and it is from the Babylonians that we can gain most information, due to their writings.

There were seven gates to the Babylonian hell of Kurnugia, each guarded by a demon sent there by Nergal, Lord of the Underworld. But he was not the true ruler – that was really his wife, the demon goddess Ereshkigal, Princess of the Kingdom of Shadows. Ereshkigal was the original ruler of hell and invited Nergal to come and join her. She offered him kingship of hell. He arrived with great pomp and ceremony – along

with his seven demons – but did so little that Ereshkigal was obliged to take over again. Until then Nergal had been the Babylonian god of destruction and war, and his main skill was in controlling Namtaru, spreader of the plague; if anyone upset Nergal, he sent Namtaru to visit them.

Once Ereshkigal had grown bored with Nergal, she cast around for a more suitable mate. Her eye alighted on Tammuz, the god of the harvest, who was also her brother-in-law. He was married to the goddess of love and lust, Ishtar. Since Ereshkigal was unable to compete with Ishtar's beauty and skills in love-making (Ishtar was also the goddess of harlots), she kidnapped Tammuz and carried him off to Kurnugia against his will. Ishtar stormed down to hell where, in order to pass through the seven gates, she had symbolically to remove an article of clothing or jewelry. She arrived, naked and vulnerable, to confront Ereshkigal, who was able to kill her easily. The god Ea then persuaded Ereshkigal to restore Ishtar to life if she would leave Tammuz in hell with her. Ishtar had to agree if she wanted to live again – but she got Ereshkigal to compromise. Tammuz now stays in hell for the winter with Ereshkigal and returns to Ishtar for the spring and summer. This was the Babylonian explanation of the seasons and, as such, includes a descent motif.

BABYLONIAN DEMON OF DISEASE AND EVIL

THE GREEK HELL

*C*LASSICAL GREECE was flourishing around the seventh century B.C., with a complex pantheon of gods and goddesses. The Greeks borrowed freely from the Babylonians, adding to and adapting the mythologies to make them their own. They believed in Hades – the Underworld – that was located a mere three yards below the surface of the earth. It was a vast cavern, a shadowy place for all the dead – good or bad. Writers such as Homer (around 850 B.C.) added to its imagery with the River Styx, that winds its way round the world of the dead nine times.

NO, NO! GO NOT TO
LETHE, NEITHER TWIST
WOLF'S-BANE, TIGHT
ROOTED, FOR ITS
POISONOUS WINE;
NOR SUFFER THY PALE
FOREHEAD TO BE KISS'D
BY NIGHTSHADE, RUBY
GRAPE OF PROSERPINE.

John Keats
On Melancholy

The ruler of Hades was Pluto, Zeus' brother, and he governed it with a merciless severity and subjected his poor guests to the most ingenious tortures. He was so savage that even the other gods were afraid of him. Pluto developed creative punishments, such as that inflicted on Sisyphus, who was made to roll a vast round stone continually up a hill. Each time he reached the top, his strength gave way and the stone rolled down again. Or the punishment meted out to Tantalus – he was kept permanently hungry and thirsty, and made to stand up to his neck in water; above his head hung fruit, but every time he tried to reach the food or water with his mouth they moved tantalizingly out of reach. These punishments usually suited the crime – Tantalus had served his own son up as part of the menu at a banquet.

Any Greek who was utterly worthless suffered
a fate worse than Hades. They were consigned to
the deep bottomless pit of Tartarus, ruled by
Kronos. Here they would suffer eternal
torment. Kronos was an earlier Greek deity
who, when replaced, had to be
demoted to the lowest place possible.
Since Hades was already occupied, he
had to be cast to an even lower hell.

The Greeks considered parricide
– the killing of a parent – one of the
most heinous sins that could be
committed, which is probably why
Oedipus was one of their most
notorious anti-heroes. As well as
parricide, the other major sin for
the Greeks was oath-breaking.

For either of these sins Greeks
were sent straight to Tartarus and
were given over to the Erinnyes –
the Daughters of Eternal Shadow.
These female demons would

PLUTO,
GOD OF THE UNDERWORLD

appear as soon as Greeks had sinned, to carry them off. The Erinnyes are
described as having serpents for hair and arriving armed with flaming

torches and whips. Once in Tartarus, sinners were tortured for eternity. Life in Hades itself was bearable by comparison. Hades was described as a place of shadowy ghosts waiting either to go on to the Elysian Fields or to be consigned to Tartarus.

However, Hades was populated with some pretty unpleasant characters – such as the Keres, hideous winged spirits of death (every soul had its own personal one). And there was Hecate herself – the triple-headed demon goddess who often frequented crossroads feasting on newly executed criminals.

BEFORE THE VERY FORECOURT AND IN THE OPENING OF THE JAWS OF HELL, GRIEF AND AVENGING CARES HAVE PLACED THEIR BEDS, AND WAN DISEASE AND SAD OLD AGE LIVE THERE, AND FEAR AND HUNGER THAT URGES TO WRONGDOING, AND SHAMING DESTITUTION, FIGURES TERRIBLE TO SEE, AND DEATH AND TOIL.

Virgil

Aeneid

Was it ever possible to escape from Hades? Well, if a soul was loved enough, someone could try to rescue them. It almost worked for Eurydice, the wife of Orpheus. She was bitten by a snake, died, and went to Hades. Orpheus went after her and enchanted Pluto with his playing of the lyre. Pluto said that Eurydice could return to the world above, on condition that Orpheus led her out without once looking back. When he was almost out, he could not resist a glance over his shoulder and so lost Eurydice for ever.

FALL OF THE REBEL ANGELS
Frans Floris 1516–70

THE EGYPTIAN HELL

*T*HE EGYPTIAN culture flourished for nearly three thousand years, and during that time its mythology naturally underwent many changes and adaptations. When the Egyptians were finally conquered by the Greeks in 332 B.C. their civilization had begun to degenerate. However, at the peak of their empire around 2000 B.C. they had developed writing and recorded, using hieroglyphics, much about death and the afterlife. These writings have been collected into the *Egyptian Book of the Dead,* from which we learn that the Ancient Egyptians divided the universe into three – heaven, earth, and the Duat, or underworld. The Duat, sometimes known as Amenti, was not originally a place of punishment but merely where the sun god, Ra, went each evening when he departed from the sky. It was peopled with the dread forces of darkness, and the Egyptians began to believe that sinners – those not believing in Ra – went there as well. They believed that the Duat must also be the domain of Ra's supernatural enemies – the goddesses of the fiery pits. Sinners and enemies of Ra, after death, were killed again by being beheaded, then were dismembered and finally their remains were burnt. However, when Ra rose each morning they were reconstituted and had to suffer the same fate again each evening at nightfall. There was no reprieve or salvation – the Duat was forever – which may account for the popularity of the cult of

ANUBIS, THE JACKAL-HEADED GOD

Osiris in the Nile valley. Followers of Osiris believed that when they died they had to stand before him and have their heart weighed on the Scales of Judgement against the feather of truth. The jackal-headed god, Anubis, did the weighing and Thoth, the baboon-headed god, recorded the result. If they failed the weighing, which they

OSIRIS, THE JUDGE
OF THE DEAD

would do if they had failed to follow the forty-two commandments of Ra, they were thrown to Am-mut – the Eater of the Dead – part lion, part crocodile, and part hippo. If they passed, they stayed forever in paradise with Osiris in the Fields of Peace (the Greeks took this theme further with their Elysian Fields). Both Osiris and Thoth were open to bribery – while someone was alive he could make offerings in any of the temples dedicated to them. Anubis seems to have been less easily swayed; so he was the chief deity to whom prayers and offerings were made at funerals. Although Osiris was the judge, it was Anubis who had to be convinced that a worthwhile life had been lived.

HEAVEN AND HELL SUPPOSE TWO DISTINCT SPECIES OF MEN, THE GOOD AND THE BAD. BUT THE GREATER PART OF MANKIND FLOAT BETWIXT VICE AND VIRTUE. WERE ONE TO GO ROUND THE WORLD WITH AN INTENTION OF GIVING A GOOD SUPPER TO THE RIGHTEOUS AND A SOUND DRUBBING TO THE WICKED, HE WOULD FREQUENTLY BE EMBARRASSED IN HIS CHOICE, AND WOULD FIND THAT THE MERITS AND DEMERITS OF MOST MEN AND WOMEN SCARCELY AMOUNT TO THE VALUE OF EITHER.

THE CHIEF SOURCE OF MORAL IDEA IS THE REFLECTION ON THE INTERESTS OF HUMAN SOCIETY. OUGHT THESE INTERESTS, SO SHORT, SO FRIVOLOUS, TO BE GUARDED BY PUNISHMENTS, ETERNAL AND INFINITE? THE DAMNATION OF ONE MAN IS AN INFINITELY GREATER EVIL IN THE UNIVERSE THAN THE SUBVERSION OF A THOUSAND MILLION KINGDOMS.

David Hume
Of the Immortality of the Soul

THE ROMAN HELL

*T*HE ROMANS knew exactly where hell was located – underneath Italy. Everything else they borrowed from the Greeks. The Roman hell was entered via a cave mouth and immediately inside this was limbo, the region where poor people who had not been buried with the appropriate rituals had to wait for a hundred years (or until someone gave them a proper burial). Then you had to cross the River Lethe, the River of Oblivion, paying the ferryman the correct fee, which would have been placed in the mouth of the deceased at the time of burial (hence the poor having to wait in limbo). The dead also had to take a tasty morsel with them to throw to Cerberus, the dread hound who guarded the gates of the underworld. Once past him, they entered the halls of Dis Pater, where they would be judged by Eita and his wife Proserpine (counterpart of the Greek Persephone). Successful candidates left by the right-hand path, that led to the Fortunate Isles (equivalent to the Greek Elysian Fields); unsuccessful ones took the left-hand path, that led to hell. This was a triple-walled fortress entered by a huge gate, on top of which perched one of the Furies. Inside, the dead would encounter three lakes, one of boiling gold, one of freezing lead, and one of iron shards. Around the edge of the lakes, demons – the Manes – would be hurling souls into them, or tossing souls between them. After being tortured like this for a while, the soul would be pounded, to get it back into some sort of shape so that it could return for another life. In the Roman hell there was also a female demon – Tuchulcha – who had burning, piercing eyes and a beak to tear the flesh. At death, the soul would be argued over by spiteful demons, led by Charun, and benevolent ones, led by Vanth. The soul was taken by whichever one won the argument about its life's worth.

> THEN STAR NOR SUN SHALL WAKEN,
>   NOR ANY CHANGE OF LIGHT:
> NOR SOUND OF WATER SHAKEN,
>   NOR ANY SOUND OR SIGHT:
> NOR WINTRY LEAVES NOR VERNAL,
>   NOR DAYS NOR THINGS DIURNAL;
> ONLY THE SLEEP ETERNAL
>   IN AN ETERNAL NIGHT.
>
> *Algernon Swinburne*
> The Garden of Proserpine

LUCRETIUS' HELL

DEMONS — LUCIFER AND EVE
Fay Pomerance

*T*HE POET LUCRETIUS lived in Rome from 99 to 55 B.C., just before the time of Christ. We have seen the Roman view of hell (pages 58–59), but not all Romans would necessarily have believed in it. Lucretius certainly did not and was most vociferous in his condemnation of such foolish beliefs.

As for Cerberus and the Furies, and the pitchy darkness and the jaws of hell belching abominable smoke and fumes — these are not and cannot be anywhere at all. But life is darkened by the fear of retribution for our misdeeds, a fear vast in proportion to their enormity, and by the penalties — imprisonment, the lash, the block, the rack, the boiling pitch, the firebrand, and the branding iron. Even though these horrors are not physically present, yet the conscience-ridden mind in terrified anticipation torments itself with its own goads and whips. It does not see how long its suffering is to be nor where its punishment can have an end. It is afraid that death may serve merely to intensify pain. So at length the life of misguided mortals becomes a Hell on earth.

As children in darkness tremble and start at everything, so we in broad daylight are oppressed by fears as baseless as those horrors which children imagine. This dread of mind can only be dispelled by an understanding of the outward form and inner workings of nature.

Why do you weep and wail over death? If the life you have lived till now has been a pleasant thing why then, you silly creature, do you not retire as a guest who has had his fill of life and take your care-free rest with a quiet mind? And if it's been distasteful why not make an end of life and labor?

THE AZTEC HELL

LAST AND CROWNING TORTURE OF ALL THE TORTURES
OF THAT AWFUL PLACE IS THE ETERNITY OF HELL.
ETERNITY! O, DREAD AND DIRE WORD. ETERNITY! WHAT
MIND OF MAN CAN UNDERSTAND IT? AND REMEMBER,
IT IS AN ETERNITY OF PAIN. EVEN THOUGH THE PAINS
OF HELL WERE NOT SO TERRIBLE AS THEY ARE, YET
THEY WOULD BECOME INFINITE, AS THEY ARE DESTINED
TO LAST FOR EVER. BUT WHILE THEY ARE EVERLASTING
THEY ARE AT THE SAME TIME, AS YOU KNOW,
INTOLERABLY INTENSE, UNBEARABLY EXTENSIVE. TO
BEAR EVEN THE STING OF AN INSECT FOR ALL ETERNITY
WOULD BE A DREADFUL TORMENT. WHAT MUST IT BE,
THEN, TO BEAR THE MANIFOLD TORTURES OF HELL FOR
EVER? FOR EVER! FOR ALL ETERNITY! NOT FOR A YEAR
OR FOR AN AGE BUT FOR EVER.

James Joyce
A Portrait of the Artist as a Young Man

*I*T IS INTERESTING to look at the concept of hell in a culture from the other side of the world, and one that had no contact with classical mythology, to see what, if any, similarities it may have. The Aztecs flourished in the area around what is now Mexico until the arrival of the Spaniards in 1520.

The rulers of the Aztec hell were Mictlantecuhtli and his wife Mictecaciuatl, and hell was called Mictlan. When the Aztecs died they were cremated with their dogs, who would carry them across a deep and wide river to arrive at Mictlan. They were also cremated with jewelry, fine clothes, perfumes, torches, and colored paper – to be used as bribes when they arrived – and the more they provided, the better afterlife they would be given. The journey to Mictlan took four years and, while the dead were being cremated, the Aztec priests would recite prayers that gave advice as to what they could expect – similar to both the Tibetan and Egyptian *Books of the Dead*. The way was beset with grisly demons and horrific adventures.

After crossing the river, bribing Mictlantecuhtli, and settling in, the dead could expect to stay for quite a while but in comparative comfort. Mictlan was a place of rest rather than torture – although the Aztecs did see it as a dark and gloomy place.

When Cortés led the Spaniards into South America it so unsettled the current ruler of the Aztecs, Montezuma, that he immediately prepared his own cremation gifts, that included the flayed skins of his slaves – and it was not too long before he needed them.

Montezuma thought that Cortés was Quetzalcoatl, the snake-bird god, returning from his journeys across the seas. Quetzalcoatl was a god of both life and death, and is often confused with Mictlantecuhtli. But he seems to have been a separate deity, although he did have considerable powers to interfere in Mictlan. Quetzalcoatl received the souls of the human sacrifices while Mictlantecuhtli presided over the souls of princes, chiefs, humble folk, and those who died of disease.

REVELATION

And there was war in heaven: Michael and his angels fought against the dragon;
and the dragon fought and his angels, but they had not the strength to win, and
no foothold was left to them in heaven. So the great dragon was thrown down, that
serpent of old that led the whole world astray, whose name is Satan, or the Devil —
thrown down to earth, and his angels with him.

And the smoke of their torment ascendeth up for ever and ever: and they have no
rest day or night, who worship the beast and his image.

Then I saw an angel coming down from heaven with the key of the abyss and a
great chain in his hands. He seized the dragon, that serpent of old, the Devil, or
Satan, and chained him up for a thousand years; he threw him into the abyss,
shutting and sealing it over him, so that he might seduce the nations no more till
the thousand years were over. After that he must be let loose for a short while.

When the thousand years are over, Satan will be let loose from his dungeon; and he
will come out to seduce the nations in the four quarters of the earth and to muster
them for battle, yes, the hosts of Gog and Magog, countless as the sands of the sea.
So they marched over the breadth of the land and laid siege to the camp of God's
people and the city that he loves. But fire came down on them from heaven and
consumed them; and the Devil, their seducer, was flung into the lake of fire
and sulphur, where the beast and the false prophet had been flung, there to be
tormented day and night for ever. Revelation 20:1–15

SATAN AROUSING THE REBEL ANGELS
William Blake 1757–1827

MODERN VISIONS OF HELL

THE CHRISTIAN HELL

OTHER RELIGIONS and cultures may have had their own ideas of hell, but it was the Christians who elevated it to an art form. Their visions of hell have influenced writers, artists, painters, and poets, as well as scholars and priests, for two thousand years. First and foremost they needed a truly magnificent ruler – who better than a fallen angel, Lucifer, the Morning Star, himself? No one knows better the exquisite pain of being excluded from heaven than one who has himself enjoyed its delights.

Originally Lucifer was thrown down from heaven into a fiery pit, where he was to wallow alone forever – or at least with the other angels who were excluded with him, and medieval scholars worked out that there were at least seven million of these to keep him company. This all occurred long before God created the earth and people.

Once Lucifer became aware of people, however, he set out to tempt them into evil ways. He began, of course, by turning himself into a serpent

THE LAST JUDGEMENT (CENTRAL PANEL)
Hieronymus Bosch c.1450–1516

CAST INTO THE FIERY
PIT OF HELL

and starting on Eve, who, as is well known, quickly succumbed. After that it was easy for the Devil, and hell soon filled up with the souls of the damned, the unfortunate, the weak, and the wicked.

And what could they expect there? Well, traditionally it was always brimstone and hell-fire. Brimstone is actually an old name for sulphur, which has a boiling point of 832°F, after which it becomes a gas. So hell was pretty hot and visually quite impressive, with the red of the fires and the yellow of the sulphur.

According to various medieval writers, hell was not under the earth but in some other dimension, and the clerics who studied it said it could contain 100 billion souls packed into a cubic mile. The Jesuit Lapped worked out that it was 200 miles across — so there was room for at least six billion, billion souls.

Once Lucifer — or Satan as he became, once installed as hell's overlord — had hell as a fully functioning place to receive the souls of the wicked and full of victims to torture, he turned his attention to capturing more souls before they had even died. The idea of selling your soul to the Devil developed during the medieval period, but there has to be a certain admiration for Satan's entrepreneurial spirit.

> FAUSTUS: AND WHAT ARE YOU THAT LIVE WITH LUCIFER?
> MEPHISTOPHELES: UNHAPPY SPIRITS THAT FELL WITH LUCIFER, CONSPIRED AGAINST OUR GOD WITH LUCIFER, AND ARE FOR EVER DAMNED WITH LUCIFER.
>
> *Christopher Marlowe*
> Dr. Faustus

He probably got the idea from the Church's sale of indulgences, that admitted the vendor straight to heaven.

In the Old Testament, hell is a place of fire without a specific ruler. In the New Testament it becomes the abode of Satan, full of weeping and the gnashing of teeth. And by the time you get to the last book in the Bible — the Book of Revelation — it has become the abominable fancy, full of chains and dragons, and infinite agony. However, it was the Synod of Bishops in Constantinople in 543 that finally set the seal on hell, when they decreed that "if anyone shall say or even think that there is an end to the torment of demons and ungodly persons, or that there ever will be an end to it, then let them be excommunicated." And they promptly excommunicated

Origen, an early Church father, for saying that he thought hell was finite. He had, unfortunately, died some 300 years earlier, but they excommunicated him anyway. Being excommunicated meant that when a person died they went straight to hell.

It was from the Middle Ages onwards that hell really started to go up in the world. Anyone wanting to lay claim to having visited it could – for no one could disprove their vision of it – so imaginations ran riot and all sorts of macabre tortures were invented to scare the ungodly and the tempted. These included being stricken with leprosy, flogged by horned demons, smeared with slime, clawed and flayed by a three-headed monster, submerged in boiling blood, covered in sores, trapped in festering ooze, sunk in boiling pitch, torn apart, eaten raw by demons, impaled, throttled, mutilated, burnt, and having your brain boiled while it was still in your head. These tortures were all designed to stop people sinning. But what were these sins that warranted such eternal agonies of unending pain? Well, there was the drinking of chocolate – that got someone sent to hell. And playing dice

THE CHRISTIAN VISION
OF HEAVEN AND HELL

or cards, as well as the more usual sins like blaspheming or being a witch, breaking any of the Commandments, not being baptized, keeping bad company, and even smoking. And if that was not bad enough, then the terrors of the Last Judgement still had to be faced.

This aspect of religious belief has caused scholars a few problems over the last two thousand years. If, when someone has died, they are judged and condemned to hell for all eternity, what happens at the Last Judgement? Are they recalled, judged again, and again thrown into hell? But hell itself is supposed to close down at the Last Judgement. Some clerics suggested that the souls of sinners would become annihilated, others that the agonies they had endured would be as nothing compared to the ones they were going to receive at the Last Judgement. Some said that everyone would be reborn, and others that only a few would – the rest would be thrown back into the fiery pit. The best explanation is probably St. Augustine's, that reasoned that hell was for souls and at the Last Judgement sinners would be reunited with their bodies, when both could be tortured forever.

Escape or redemption from the Christian hell has always been denied to sinners – once incarcerated in hell, there was simply no chance of escape or redemption.

THE JEWISH HELL

*H*ISTORICAL EVIDENCE indicates that the Jewish nation originated in Ur in Chaldea around 1900 B.C. The Jewish people migrated considerably, including time spent in both Egypt and Mesopotamia, until settling in the Holy Land around 539 B.C. During these periods of migration their myths changed and developed according to where they settled.

The Jewish concept of hell started out originally as a place of shadows and ghosts – Sheol – where the dead wandered about forever, aimlessly and without punishment. There was no heaven or reunion with God – after death there was nothing at all except a grey place of animated corpses. The general impression was simply one of dreariness, and there was no mention of an immortal soul or of life everlasting. Later a concept of the final day of judgement crept in, as depicted in the Book of Daniel:

> *And many of them that sleep in the dust of the earth shall awake, some to everlasting life and some to shame and everlasting contempt.*

One of the purposes of myth and religion in many cultures was to help the leaders control their people with threats of damnation. Sheol underwent a transformation to Gehenna – the place of fire. It is probable that it was named after the place just outside Jerusalem where the household rubbish, including the bodies of criminals and animals, was burnt.

Gehenna was not ruled over by any particular deity but came under the direct control of Yahweh, God. There was, however, some chance of escape or redemption. Adulterers had only to endure the hell-fire for a period of twelve months, after which they could go to heaven. Real sinners – those who had shamed their neighbours publicly or who had not obeyed the phylactery (scriptures written on slips of parchment and worn in a box on the left arm or forehead) – were put into the hell-fire for twelve months, at the end of which they were annihilated and simply ceased to be.

The worst punishment, though, was reserved for Christians, informers, and those who despised the words of the rabbis (Jewish priests), who were to endure the hell-fires for all eternity.

Anyone who renounced their Jewish faith had to stay in Gehenna until they recanted and, once accepted back into the faith, could go on to heaven.

In some versions of Jewish belief there are also those who will be punished by plague instead of fire – these are the wicked, the readers of foreign books, sorcerers, and anyone given over to excess pleasure.

HOW YOU HAVE FALLEN FROM HEAVEN, BRIGHT MORNING STAR, FELLED TO THE EARTH, SPRAWLING HELPLESS ACROSS THE NATIONS! YOU THOUGHT IN YOUR OWN MIND, I WILL SCALE THE HEAVENS; I WILL SET MY THRONE HIGH ABOVE THE STARS OF GOD, I WILL SIT ON THE MOUNTAIN WHERE THE GODS MEET IN THE FAR RECESSES OF THE NORTH. I WILL RISE ABOVE THE CLOUD BANKS AND MAKE MYSELF LIKE THE MOST HIGH. YET SHALL YOU BE BROUGHT DOWN TO SHEOL, TO THE DEPTHS OF THE ABYSS.

Isaiah 14:12

There is little in the way of description of the actual geography of Gehenna, or of its location. It seems to have been seen merely as a place filled with fire, although in Enoch we find a brief hint of what is to be expected:

It had all manner of tortures; cruel darkness, dim gloom. There was no light but that of murky fire. It had a fiery river and the whole place is everywhere fire, everywhere frost and ice, thirst and shivering, while the fetters are cruel, and the angels fearful and merciless, bearing sharp weapons and merciless tortures.

YOUR BEAUTY MADE YOU ARROGANT, YOU MISUSED YOUR WISDOM TO INCREASE YOUR DIGNITY. I FLUNG YOU TO THE GROUND, I LEFT YOU THERE, A SIGHT FOR KINGS TO SEE. SO GREAT WAS YOUR SIN IN YOUR WICKEDNESS THAT YOU DESECRATED YOUR SANCTUARIES. SO I KINDLED A FIRE WITHIN YOU, AND IT DEVOURED YOU. I LEFT YOU AS ASHES ON THE GROUND FOR ALL TO SEE. ALL AMONG THE NATIONS WHO KNEW YOU WERE AGHAST: YOU CAME TO A FEARFUL END AND SHALL BE NO MORE FOR EVER.
Ezekiel 28:17

It seems strange, the idea of both frost and fire being everywhere, but it is a theme that recurs often in many belief systems about hell – probably because the two extremes of temperature were deeply feared by primitive peoples.

As the early Christians developed their own ideas about hell, these were incorporated into Jewish belief until by about the fourth century A.D. there was little to distinguish the two religions' beliefs – except for Lilith. In Jewish belief she was Adam's first wife and she left him because he insisted on being on top during sex. For this terrible disobedience she was banished to the "aery void," where she became Satan's principal helper and led the "succubi" – fearful female demons who seduced men in their sleep.

THE GREAT DAY OF HIS WRATH
C.Mottram fl.1876–1903

THE BUDDHIST HELL

*B*UDDHISM was founded by Gotama Buddha in India around the sixth century B.C. It quickly spread throughout the whole of Asia, although it never replaced Hinduism in India itself. The Buddha preached that "karma" — what is done in one life being carried forward as merit or burden into the next life — was the fundamental principle of life. A soul could only escape the cycle of reincarnation by becoming enlightened and thus going to Nirvana after death. For the Buddha there was no hell, except the one of this life. He saw all of life as suffering, and taught that it should be the aim of each human being to seek both to alleviate that universal suffering and to attain enlightenment.

Since the Buddha's death Buddhism has gone through many changes and additions as it has spread from country to country. Some Buddhists now believe in the Buddha as a deity; others do not. In some Buddhist sects there is a well-defined hierarchy of gods and demons while others have none.

Some branches of Buddhism even believe that there is not one hell but eight. One of these eight hells is to be endured in the space between death and being reborn, depending on our sins:

SAMJIVA — The Hell of Repetition: for anyone killing any living creature — for 500 years

KALA-SUTRA — The Hell of Black Coils: for thieves — for 1,000 years

SAMGHATA — The Crowded Hell: for sexual deviants — for 2,000 years

RAURAVA – The Screaming Hell: for drunkards – for 4,000 years

MAHA- RAURAVA – The Great Screaming Hell: for liars – for 8,000 years

TAPANA – The Burning Hell: for those holding wrong opinions – for 16,000 years

PRA-TAPANA – The Great Burning Heat Hell: for those who sexually abuse monks or nuns – for half a kalpa

AVICI – The Hell of No End: for murderers – lasting a whole kalpa.

A "kalpa" lasts the length of time it takes for a bird to sharpen its beak on a granite cube measuring a mile on each side – the bird only visits the granite block once every 10,000 years – and when the block has completely worn away, then one kalpa has passed.

Some of the Tibetan Buddhists – the Ladaks – believe however that there is no need of hell, for sinners are immediately reincarnated in the next life as marmots – a type of rodent that burrows underground. They consider that punishment enough, no matter what your sins. This is a similar belief to that of the native Gallinomero people of California, who believed that sinners return as coyotes.

The Mahayana Buddhists of Tibet believe that hell only lasts for forty-nine days. This is the length of time between a soul leaving a dying person and being incarnated in the womb of its next life. During this time, according to the *Tibetan Book of the Dead*, the soul faces many demons and frightening hallucinations. These are to test the purity of the soul. If it has practised Buddhism during its life, then it will not be frightened and can go past these demonic apparitions to Nirvana. If the soul has not been prepared by the correct religious practices, it will take fright and seek refuge in the warmth and comfort of a new existence on earth.

During the forty-nine days, prayers, in the form of spiritual guidance, should be read aloud over the recently deceased to help the soul become free from existence. These prayers take the form of instruction such as:

O nobly-born, if thou recognize not, and be frightened, the Lord of Death will shine forth. When such thought forms emanate be thou not afraid nor terrified; the body which now thou possessest being a mental body of karmic propensities, though slain and chopped to bits cannot die. Because thy body is in reality one of voidness thou needst not fear. The Lord of Death is also an emanation of thine own intellect; it is not made of matter; voidness cannot harm voidness. Thus knowing all this, all the fear and terror is self-dissipated; and merging in the state of atonement Buddhahood is obtained.

The demons that accompany the Lord of Death – known as Yama-Raja – are the "gshed-ma" – the tormenting furies, and should the soul have pursued a truly wicked life, they will chase it down to be born in hell:

...lands of gloom, black houses and white houses, and black holes in the earth, and black roads along which one hath to go will appear. If one goeth there one will enter Hell; and suffering unbearable pains of heat and cold one will be very long in getting out of it. Go not there.

Some of the punishments to be encountered in the Tibetan hell include: having a gshed-ma pour spoonfuls of molten metal into a woman condemned for prostitution; being crushed by a gigantic sacred book,

DEATH — DANCING SKELETONS
Indian painting mid-19th century

which is the punishment for not reading the scriptures carefully; being quartered and stuck on spikes, the punishment for practising witchcraft; being sawn in two lengthways, for murderers; and being boiled alive in cauldrons for resisting being judged. Yama-Raja, the Lord of Death, does the judging. He counts out a soul's good deeds as white pebbles and the bad deeds as black pebbles. If there is more of one color you go to heaven (an excess of white pebbles) or to hell (an excess of black ones). The soul's punishment in hell will depend on how many excess black pebbles it has. The hell of the Mahayana Buddhists of Tibet is a limited one — there is always hope of redemption, either through repentance, time served, or divine intervention from the Buddha himself, who has occasionally been known to barter for the freedom of a soul with Lord Yama-Raja.

THE CHINESE HELL

HE TWO PRINCIPAL belief systems of China — Taoism and Buddhism — have both borrowed extensively from each other's ideas about hell, so that they have become amalgamated into a complex image from which it is difficult to separate the two strands. Taoists hold that hell is ruled by the Yan-Wang, the Supreme Master of Hell, who presides over the eighteen levels of hell. This is a good example of hell reflecting the class system of its believers. China had a distinct hierarchy and the eighteen levels represented the eighteen different classes of people and professions at that time.

In each level the soul can expect a different torture, depending on its sins and, more importantly, its occupation during life. At the point of death Yan-Wang's two principal helpers appear to carry off the newly deceased.

TIBETAN TANKA MANDALA
Early twentieth century

These are Niu-t'ou, the Ox Demon, and Ma-mien, the Horse Demon. Gods from heaven will also be present and will squabble over the soul until one side wins (in a way similar to the Roman belief). This process can take between seven and forty-nine days, which is why the Chinese delay burial for so long — it would not do to be buried before the fate of the soul had been decided.

If the demons win the contest, then the soul is taken off to hell. Once there, it is assigned to its level and to its own particular form of torture. If the dead person had been a sinful mandarin, they would expect to have to swallow molten gold and silver. A publisher making too much in the way of profits would be impaled on spikes, and a grave-robber would be hurled into a mountain of fire and boiled in oil.

During all these tortures the soul would be tormented and made to suffer unendurable agonies by demons who had themselves once been alive. They had all had the same occupation – that of politician – and have no hope of reprieve. They are usually depicted as having two horns on the front of their heads and carrying a trident to jab sinners with. Sound familiar?

Sinners can bribe their way out of hell by getting their living relatives to burn paper money. Of course, the politician-demons had no real incentive to let them out, as they were never going to get to spend any of the money.

Buddhists have similar levels of hell and similar punishments, but a fairer and more humane method of redemption: the Bodhisattva Ti-tsang was a young Buddhist monk who made a vow to save all sinners' souls. He dedicated all his subsequent incarnations to this end and accumulated so much merit that he is allowed, by the Buddha, to visit hell from time to time and rescue any souls who are either there by mistake or who have truly repented.

There is another way out of hell. If someone dies an unnatural death, then they are allowed to persuade or trick someone into taking their place and they can go free. The only condition is that their replacement has to

have died of the same cause as they did. Thus if they have been murdered, they have to find a similar victim, and if they have drowned they have to find someone who has also drowned. After three years in hell they are allowed to return to the place where they died, and they can actually kill some poor unsuspecting victim in a like manner. This is why the Chinese avoid places where there has been a death, especially an accident or a suicide, since they do not want to get tricked into taking someone else's place in hell.

Hell, for the Chinese, can never be eternal because the soul will always be required to return to earth and be incarnated again. However, souls may have to spend a considerable time in hell — especially if they have been found guilty of a really wicked sin such as having worn purple clothes, which only the Emperor was allowed to do.

THE SIX DIVISIONS OF THE WORLD
early 20th-century Tibetan mandala

THE JAPANESE HELL

HE ANCIENT RELIGION of Japan was Shinto, which concerned itself with nature spirits. Shinto had no real concept of hell – dead people's souls went to heaven – but there was a region under the earth, Yomi-T'su-Kuni, the "land of darkness," where all wicked things lived. These wicked things were personifications of the calamities that affect people at one time or another – illness, misfortune, accidents, epidemics, misery, poverty, and curses. These afflictions, rising up to annoy humans, took the form of demons – usually female – who were known as the Shiko-Me, the "ugly ones," but they could usually be deflected with an appropriate prayer or an offering to Kamu-Nahobi, the god-who-puts-things-right.

Once Buddhism had gained a hold in Japan, around 500 A.D., the concept of hell expanded. It became Jigoku, the "ground under the ground." It was made up of eight worlds of fire and eight worlds of ice, and was ruled by Emma-O, the Great Judge of Hell, who had a mere 8,000 demons, the Oni, to help him. Once dead, the soul was taken to him by a horse-faced or ox-faced demon (borrowed from the Chinese) for judging, but Emma-O was a stern and ferocious judge. There was no chance of fooling him into believing that they had led a better life than he thought, because he was the owner of a splendid magic mirror in which was reflected not the person's physical image but their sins.

Once judgement, and its respective torture, was given, the soul was in hell until sufficient prayers had been said for its salvation by its descendants.

Alternatively, it could appeal to the Buddha, who would send a bodhisattva, a Buddhist living god, to hear its case. If it could persuade the bodhisattva that it had truly repented, it could be reborn and have another chance at life.

> *Judging by pictures*
> *Hell looks more interesting*
> *Than that other place.*

Old Japanese proverb

The Japanese have their own version of the descent motif that parallels the Greek myth of Orpheus and Eurydice: the god Izanagi was extremely sad when his wife, the goddess Izanami, died in childbirth (producing the god of fire, Ho-Masubi), and he resolved to go down into hell and retrieve her. He met her at the entrance to hell and was naturally overjoyed to see her. Izanami, however, was not too pleased to see him and refused to go back with him, since she had tasted of the food of hell and found it to her liking.

She suggested that she go and ask the advice of Emma-O, and Izanagi was to wait there and, under no circumstances, to enter hell. He disobeyed and went in. The first thing he saw was Izanami's body rotting and riddled with worms. She then swore he had humiliated her and set the Shiko-Me on him. He fled pursued by the ugly demons and by the eight gods of Thunder. These are not the gods of heavenly thunder, but rather the gods of underground thunder – the Nari-Kami or "earthquake gods."

受過各種之苦到此仍照惡加刑

司阿鼻大地獄十惡之徒

Izanagi managed to block off the gate of hell with a huge rock but found that Izanami was also outside. They refused to be reconciled and were divorced. After that Izanagi became a recluse.

As the various sects of Buddhism developed in Japan, so too did the many beliefs about what happens after death. According to the Jodo-Shinshu Buddhists, after death there is only the paradise of Nirvana or the hell of being reincarnated into this world. Only by living a pure and holy life can we escape from this living hell.

THE DEMONIC OVERSEERS IN THE BUDDHIST HELL
fresco in the Tiger Balm Gardens

THE HERE AND NOW OF HELL

CHANGING IMAGES OF HELL

THOMAS MANN, writing his version of *Dr. Faustus* in 1948, set it in Nazi Germany, and for many of us the two World Wars have been vision enough of a hell here and now. Although most theologians would now discount the older versions of hell as a place of brimstone and fire, hell – as a metaphor – continues to remain an extremely powerful image. Victor Sinclair Blackwood, a powerful and charismatic magician, wrote in 1925 that hell was probably closed, but that the merest threat of it was sufficient to "frighten most people and challenge those who would be foolhardy!"

Are we still frightened by visions of hell? Drug addicts and schizophrenics would

EVERY COMPASSION, EVERY GRACE, EVERY SPARING, EVERY LAST TRACE OF CONSIDERATION FOR THE INCREDULOUS, IMPLORING OBJECTION "THAT YOU VERILY CANNOT DO SO UNTO A SOUL:" IT IS DONE, IT HAPPENS, AND INDEED WITHOUT BEING CALLED TO ANY RECKONING IN WORDS; IN SOUNDLESS CELLAR, FAR DOWN BENEATH GOD'S HEARING, AND HAPPENS TO ALL ETERNITY.

Thomas Mann
Dr. Faustus

probably claim to have a more intimate knowledge of hell and its imagery than most, but for the rest of us hell remains a sufficiently powerful archetype to influence our thinking – we may not believe, but we don't want to go there. We may not actively conjure up visions of hell, but we are still sufficiently in touch with primeval instincts to think twice before we sin – lest we endanger our mortal souls. Even if we subscribe to no organized religion and prefer the alternative of karma and reincarnation, we still maintain a lurking and healthy respect for the concept of eternal damnation and punishment. We may not actually believe, but we will make sure that we do not challenge the Devil – just in case.

As we approach the second millennium, the world as we know it is coming to an end. What awaits us beyond this century? Many prophets and seers have predicted a cataclysmic end of the world – but may it not be a destruction of darkness and superstition? Science has worked hard to convince us that all in the known universe can be explained – there is no God. Perhaps, as we move into the twenty-first century, there will be an end to argument and reasoning, and science and magic will go forward in a spirit of harmony. We can have logic and wonder, belief and reasoning. The

GOD DID NOT SPARE THE ANGELS WHO SINNED,
BUT CONSIGNED THEM IN CHAINS TO THE
DARKNESS IN THE PITS OF HELL, WHERE THEY
ARE RESERVED FOR JUDGEMENT.

The Second Letter of Peter

THE SIXTH PALACE OF HELL
Fay Pomerance

only end will be one of division, and the balance of the universe will be restored – heaven and hell will reunite and sinners will be forgiven.

This is an age of self-responsibility – we can no longer blame the Devil for tempting us, or ourselves for giving in to temptation. We just *are* ourselves, and we forgive ourselves if we fall from grace in moments of weakness. We no longer expect to be perfect. As science opens up the might and vastness of the universe, we become aware of the smallness and fragility of humankind. That the good and evil forces of the universe should seek to do battle, using us as pawns, seems increasingly ridiculous. And yet evil is still alive, and if present must emanate from somewhere. The old "sins" have all now been forgotten and the only true sin is that we stood by and did nothing while someone, somewhere, suffered. We know when we are not doing enough, and punish ourselves. The old hell of torment and damnation is not needed in the modern hell of guilt and self-analysis. We know we are weak and uncaring, and have to struggle to rise higher than the demons of old who taunted us. We can become "superhuman" and seize power when we choose. Even Friedrich Nietzsche, who willingly abandoned God, was a believer.

No! come back,
With all your torments!
Oh come back
To the last of all solitaires!
All the streams of my tears
Run their course for you!
And the last flame of my heart –
It burns up to you!
Oh come back
My unknown god!
My pain!
My last – happiness.

Friedrich Nietzsche
Thus Spake Zarathustra

FURTHER READING

An Anthology of the Great Myths and Epics by Donna Rosenberg
(NTC Publishing, 1992).

The Bhagavad Gita, edited by Swami Chidbhavananda
(Independent Publishing, 1969).

Chinese Mythology by Derek Walters (Diamond Books, 1995).

Classic Myth & Legend by A. R. Hope Moncrieff
(Gresham Publishing, 1927).

The Devil and all His Works by Dennis Wheatley (Arrow, 1971).

Devils, Demons & Witchcraft by Ernst and Johanna Lehner
(Dover Publications, 1971).

The Dictionary of Greek and Roman Mythology by David Kravits
(New English Library, 1975).

Egyptian Book of the Dead, edited by Sir Wallis Budge
(Routledge & Kegan Paul, 1951).

Encyclopaedia of Gods by Michael Jordan (Kyle Cathie, 1992).

The Encyclopaedia of Horror by Richard Davies (Octopus Books, 1982).

The Encyclopaedia of Mythology by Eric Flaum (Magna Books, 1995).

The Encyclopaedia of Myths and Legends by Stuart Gordon (Headline, 1993).

The History of Hell by Alice K. Turner (Harcourt Brace, 1993).

The Illustrated Encyclopaedia of Myths and Legends by Arthur Cotterell
(Marshall Editions, 1989).

The Norse Tarot by Clive Barrett (Aquarian Press, 1989).

North American Indians by Lewis Spence (Studio Editions, 1994).

Orientalism by Edward W. Said (Penguin, 1985).

The Poisoned Embrace by Lawrence Osborne (Bloomsbury, 1993).

Teach Yourself Mythology by Roni Jay (Hodder & Stoughton, 1996).

The Viking Saga by Peter Brent (Weidenfeld & Nicolson, 1975).

World Mythology by Roy Willis (Duncan Baird Publishing, 1993).

ACKNOWLEDGMENTS

The author would like to thank Roni Jay for the use of her extensive and wonderful library for the research for this book; thanks also to the many writers and artists who have gone before to chart the geography of hell; and special thanks to Bal and Stephanie della Croce.